AF615492

THREE FABLES

Mary Barnard

THREE FABLES

Mary Barnard

BREITENBUSH
Portland, Oregon

First Printing 2 3 4 5 6 7 8 9 10

Library of Congress Cataloging In Publication Data

Barnard, Mary
Three fables.

Selections originally published in the Kenyon review, winter 1948.
1. Fables, American. I. Title.
PS3503.A5825T5 1983 813'.54 83-19719
ISBN 0-932576-20-6
ISBN 0-932576-21-4 (pbk.)

Breitenbush Books is grateful to the Metropolitan Arts Commission of Portland, Oregon, and to Marylhurst Education Center of Marylhurst, Oregon, for grants that made this publication possible.

Breitenbush Books are published for James Anderson by Breitenbush Publications, P.O. Box 02137, Portland, Oregon 97202.

Cover art by Edy Murphey, 'Beacon Rock'
Additional production information contained in colophon

Manufactured in the U.S.A.

PREFACE

Five years ago this December Breitenbush published its first title, *I Want To Be A Crowd* by Peter Sears, a supplementary text for teaching poetry in the schools.

What began as a fanciful and blissfully ignorant whim of four Reed College students has grown into a beautiful, exotic, multi-blossomed flower that consumes currency of large denominations at an astonishing rate. Throughout the past four years, as my three friends went on to medical school, dental school, and law school, I have been constantly reminded of the words of Walter Wolf on auto racing. His formula for making a small fortune, he said, was to take a large one and go racing. The same can be said of literary publishing: the rewards are no less exciting and the work can be as life-threatening to the psyche of the publisher/editor as racing is to the body of the Grand Prix driver. But what a ride! And as the years go by you become more thankful for friends and the mixture of skill and good fortune that allow you to continue while navigating through the debris of both the novice and veteran.

It is fitting that Breitenbush should celebrate its fifth anniversary with the publication of *Three Fables* by Mary Barnard. Her *Collected Poems* was the second title we published and the first to give the Press a taste of critical acclaim. In many ways it set the standards by which I have since operated Breitenbush. In brief, we have selected quality manuscripts of modern or contemporary literature (usually poetry) that might not be published without our initiative and then presented these manuscripts in a form that clearly demonstrates our respect for the work. Attention to page design, typography, acid-free papers, sewn bindings, and complete cloth covers have become as important to the Press as the selection of manuscripts. *Three Fables* represents all the considerations of Breitenbush.

During 1982-83 I taught a full-year class at Marylhurst College in Portland, Oregon, on the fundamentals of book publishing. It was my aim to give preparation, and a sense of caution, to the prospective publisher, author, and printer, and maybe communicate some of the joy of working with books. Our course project became this book. So let it signify the survival and success of Breitenbush Publications and the thrill of being involved with the making and reading of books which might not have otherwise found their way into print.

James Anderson
October 1st, 1983

I

FABLE FROM VANTAGE

NOW THERE WAS this road zigzagging through country hot as hell – all coulees and rimrock and not enough grass to pasture sheep – and there were three travelers on the road, not together, you understand, but one after the other, too far apart for one to see what happened to the one before him. And all three travelers were hot and tired and hungry, sore in their feet from so many rocks, and wobbly in the knees from the stiff grades up and then down, up and then down, and sunburned, but hopeful. They always thought that things would look better from the top of the next ridge. Finally the road came out on the edge of a bluff that formed one side of a great river gorge. Straight below on the bank of the blue river stood a tower, and from the tower two bridges to the opposite shore made a shape like a V. The one to the left, to the south, led to a beautiful garden spot like fine irrigated land, green and lush with orchards and happy with little summer houses. The other, to the right, to the north, led to a shale beach about two feet wide and four feet long, and from that the cliffs went straight up – I mean *really* straight up. Of course there must have been a foothold in the rocks, or the bridge wouldn't have led over there, would it? But it didn't look that way.

The first traveler came to the edge of the gorge and looked down, and first he saw the garden spot. His heart leapt up so hard it hurt in his chest, but when he saw the bridge to the north, he had misgivings. He hurried to the bottom of the hill, and all the way he could smell ripe strawberries and broiling trout. At the bank of the river, he found that the road went straight into the tower. Inside there were two doors, apparently opening upon the two bridges, and the one to the left had a sign on it saying No Exit, and the sign on the one on the right said Exit. The first traveler had been well-educated – that is, he could read and his obedience to the letter of the Law was deeply ingrained. So he groaned, as well he might. Then he tightened his belt, adjusted his knapsack, and, with a cry of "Excelsior!" opened the door marked EXIT – and found himself not on a bridge, but in a small room with cobwebs over the windows. "How odd," he said. "This is certainly not what I was led to expect." He thought that there was no way out of the room, but in that he was mistaken. Suddenly a trapdoor opened under his feet, and he found himself hurtling into the river.

"Anyway," he said to himself, "I have the satisfaction of knowing that I did what was right." And he died as peacefully as most men, and his body rolled on the bed of the river.

The second traveler was also educated – at least he could read, and his impulse, usually, was to obey the letter of the Law because he had found out by bitter experience that you were likely to be in for trouble if you didn't. When he came to the tower, he stood staring at the two doors, and groaned and deliberated within himself. He thought that after all, he had seen the garden, but he had no idea what was at the top of the cliffs; and that the unknown danger that he risked if he disobeyed the Law was probably no worse than the known effort of getting up those cliffs. All the way down the hill he had sniffed the fragrance of apricots and frying frog hams that had been wafted to him across the river. "Damned if I will," he said, and flung open the door marked NO EXIT. Immediately he found himself in the small room with cobwebs over the windows.

"Well, I might have expected something like this," he muttered. "In fact, I did expect it." At that moment the trapdoor opened under his feet and he found himself hurtling into the river. "Well, I asked for it," said the traveler with a certain amount of satisfaction, and died as peacefully as most men, and his body rolled on the bed of the river.

The third traveler, when he arrived in front of the doors, was in a sad case, because he had never learned to read. He studied one door, and then the other. He saw that there were strange marks on the two doors, and saw that they were not the same. He studied the tracks on the dusty floor of the tower and saw that one man had passed through one door and one through the other, very recently. He shouted, but only an echo came back to him from the rafters. He considered that the way towards the south had looked much pleasanter – so much pleasanter that he felt dubious about going that way because he had learned that appearances on the road were often deceiving. The fragrance of apples and roasting pheasant argued with the blisters which he had acquired by trusting those appearances. So he thought and thought. "I'm probably a fool if I do this," he said to himself. "But on the other hand, maybe I'm a bigger fool if I do that. Oh dear."

Finally he realized that he had to do something. He threw himself on one door (either one, I really don't remember which), and found himself in the room with cobwebs over the windows, and said, "Dammit, why didn't I get an education and learn to read, and then I wouldn't be in pickles like this. Oh what a fool I am! Why didn't I take the other door?" Then the trapdoor opened under his feet, and as he hurtled into the river, he screamed with despair: "If I'd only taken the other door! If I'd only taken – glug – the other – glug-glug" and he died as miserably as any man ever did. In fact, I can't think of a worse end.

II

ASCENT WITH CHORUS

DON'T ASK ME why anybody *wants* to climb that rock tied to anybody else. All I know is, every now and then, somebody does. This couple I was telling you about had that idea, and if you never had it, you don't understand. They turned up bright and early one morning, he with the blankets, and she with the lunch in a knapsack. They had alpenstocks and a rope to tie themselves together. From the way the two Old Timers leaning against the store front swapped looks and spat in the dust, you could see they understood all right, and didn't think much of the idea either. As the couple walked away into the fir grove at the foot of the rock, the Old Timers watched her plump little rear rolling in the jaunty blue slacks. "Women!" said one of them, with a deep, disagreeable belly laugh.

An old Granny sitting in a rocker on the porch cracked her knuckles and looked after them with a disapproving glint in her eye. "Cain't tell which is which," she mumbled toothlessly, but she happened to be looking at the man at the time.

The couple walked side by side, holding hands, up through the fir grove. It was a beautiful morning and they were very excited. When they came to the foot of the rock itself, they knotted the rope tightly around their waists and began to climb, he in the lead. They were above the top of the trees in no time, and could see a creek falling into the river, and the river itself widening the higher they climbed. It was fun to feel the tug of the other person at the end of the rope, sometimes a little lift, sometimes a little possessive pull back, and sometimes just a kind of misunderstanding about which way they were going which made them both laugh a lot.

Then the sun began to get them. There was no shade you could call shade on that side of the rock, and no foothold on the other side except near the top, and by afternoon, when they got there, the sun would be around on that side. Of course they couldn't even see the top by this time because the sides of the rock were so straight up and down. They hadn't any idea how far they really had to go or they might have turned around and gone back then and there. They were sweaty and breathless and their muscles ached. He had on a new sport shirt with hardly any sleeves and his white arms were turning pink. She tanned naturally without using Skol or anything, but she already had the tact not to mention it. Though both of them wanted a drink of cold water the worst way, they hadn't yet come to the point of talking about impossible wants to each other, much less blaming the other one when what they wanted couldn't be had.

But once in a while he said, "You're pulling back on me all the time. Can't you come a little faster?"

"Look," she said finally. "I pull back on you because I'm on the bottom end of this rope. You pull up on me because you're on the top end. If you want to change places, you'll see quick enough that I won't pull back on you."

What he answered to that, he muttered to a

hunk of rock in front of his face, so she didn't hear it, but she had a good idea what it was.

"I suppose you've still got the lunch," he said after a while.

"Lunch? What lunch? Oh!"

"For crying out loud, aren't you carrying the lunch?"

"Oh, it's in the knapsack. I just wasn't thinking about it at the moment. You don't want to eat now, do you?"

"Of course not. But I should think you'd have it on your mind."

"Yes, dear. But I have to think about where I'm putting my feet."

"You don't have to think about where you are putting your feet. You just put your feet where I put mine and you'll be all right."

"O.K., darling."

"That's the girl."

Up they climbed till they came to a ledge where she stood a little below, but near some very promising footholds. "Look," she said. "I think I'll try it this way."

"Hey!" he yelled. "What the hell do you think you're doing?"

"But you say I'm always pulling back on you. You follow me for a while, and I won't."

"You'd get in my way. Come down from there. You don't know anything about climbing."

"I do too. I took mountain-climbing in college."

"Classes in mountain-climbing for girls ought to be prohibited. You took mountain-climbing in college and you had to ask your mother this morning how many pieces of bread to use in a sandwich."

"Well, it only took her a minute to tell me, and suppose the rope broke and you fell off and here I was all by myself and didn't know how to get down again. I'd starve."

"Oh, so you're supposing I'm going to fall off and be killed, are you?" he cried, very rightly indignant that she could even bear to think of such a thing. *He* couldn't.

"Darling, of course you won't. But after all, it could happen –"

Naturally the more she tried to explain, the worse it sounded to him.

The Old Timers, who had remained motionless, leaning against the store front, were watching the progress of the two little dots on the rock.

"Settin there havin an argyment," said one.

"She was a-goin ahead of him," said the other, "but he ain't a-goin to let her."

"Settin argifyin," the first one said. "He ought to take and crack her head agen the rock. That'd learn her."

"Ain't got the strenth in his arms," mumbled the Granny.

"Haw!" said the first one again. "It's the way I treated my old woman. They like it. Take and crack her head agen the rock."

"Never used mine thatta way," said the second one. "She was a delicate critter, she was. Carried her smellin salts all the way up, and never had time to get em out of her pocket. Ever time we come to a bad place, she fainted dead away in my arms." He held out his arms like this.

The first one shook his head. "Tch, tch. Wouldn't know how to deal with that kind of woman."

"Why I married ye," chuckled Granny, taking out her corncob pipe. She touched a scar on her forehead thoughtfully. "Damn ye," she added.

Up on the ledge, the couple were so heated by

their quarrel that they had almost forgotten the sun, which still blazed away.

"I suppose," he said, "you'd like to take off the rope and go on up by yourself."

"For a plugged nickel, I would," said she.

That brought them to their senses.

"Look," she said. "It's not that important. Let's go on, or it'll be dark before we get to the top."

So they went on, he in the lead. They climbed in silence, but she was thinking all the time, and not about the lunch, and not about where to put her feet. Then she began to talk.

"Imagine," she said, "trying to climb this rock with that ape I used to run around with. We'd have been dashed to bits before now."

He grunted.

She sagged on the rope from time to time. He waited for her.

"Oh dear," she said. "I'm afraid your arms are getting dreadfully sunburned. Didn't we bring any Unguentine? Oh! it hurts me to *look* at it." She covered her eyes with her hands and as a result almost fell off the rock.

"It's nothing," he said gruffly. "Don't worry

about me. Just keep climbing. That's the girl."

She screamed. He gripped hard to a bush sprouting from a crevice, expecting to feel her weight dangling from the end of the rope, but she was only sagging against it again. He looked around in annoyance. "What is it now?"

"Oh, this is dreadful. I just remembered I forgot to put the little green onions in the lunch!"

"Hell's bells!" he said. "You have to think about the lunch at a moment like this, and you not only have to think about it, you have to scream about it!"

"But sweetheart, I know you *love* little green onions."

"It really isn't that important," he said wearily, and they went on.

"Look, dear," she said, "I think if you headed a little to the right, now –"

"I *am* heading to the right," he said. "I headed to the right back there, and I'm still going to the right."

"Oh, of course," she said. "I didn't notice."

"Probably thinking about little green onions," he said patronizingly. "Never mind, as long as we're roped together you'll get there all right."

"Ooooh!" she said. "Look down there! It's practically straight down."

"Your grandmother," he said, "would never have dared look down there. She would probably have fainted."

"*My* Grandma," she retorted, "had enough muscle to come up this rock like a breeze, in three flannel petticoats, too, and I never heard Grandpa complain about it. Climbing this rock was really tough in his day."

After that a silence fell, and it was only by crying over her blisters that she got a smile out of him again.

In spite of everything, they reached the top in good time, just before sunset. They spread out their blankets and opened the lunch.

"What sandwiches!" he exclaimed. "It's a pity you learned so much useless stuff in college and nothing from your mother."

"I learned a lot from my mother," she said, calm as you please. "I just didn't notice at the time – not until I needed it."

"You apparently didn't think you needed it when you made these sandwiches."

"Nope," she said, licking her fingers.

They spent the night on top of the rock and got back to the bottom in the late afternoon of the next day. The Old Timers were still, or again, leaning against the store front.

"See you made it," they remarked in an off-hand way.

"Sure," said the man and the girl in a breath.

The Old Timers looked after her as she trotted off down the path where a little faded sign said LADIES.

The man rubbed his mid-section, which had been chafed raw by the rope. "Women!" he said, shaking his head. Then he laughed.

The Old Timers spat in the dust. "Reckon they haven't changed much," they said, and chuckled.

Granny, rocking on the porch, cracked her knuckles and sighed.

III

FIRE

SHE WAS WEARING a fur coat, the mink her husband had given her for Christmas, and under that a suit of Cheviot tweed, and under that a jerkin knit of coarse red wool with a design of blue and white flowers, and under that a long-sleeved flannel blouse, and under that a suit of long underwear bought when she was in college, for skiing. She had worn it but once. Wool was so itchy, she had said. In addition, she wore a triangular woolen scarf tied around her head and angora mittens. Her feet were in fleece-lined boots, and she was wrapped besides, from her feet to her waist, in two steamer blankets. There she sat by the cold radiator. Her husband, who had set out on a trip of exploration to the basement, had been gone for three hours.

The city seemed ominously silent. Twenty stories up, traffic noises were diminished, but a confused hum and a scattered hooting had always been audible. Today, there were only tiny scratching sounds from far below, as of a few orphaned ants.

All her self-control was necessary to keep her from going again to touch the radiator. She knew the feel of it by now. The cold of the cast iron had eaten into her flesh. The metal window frames were even colder – so cold that they were lightly fleeced where she had touched them with her angora mittens. Through her fogging breath she stared at the Gauguin that hung on the opposite wall. She burrowed into her wrappings and tried to concentrate on the tropical colors of the painting and on the brown half-naked bodies that looked so warm. No use. Shuddering, she saw only naked skin exposed to the cold. She had had that feeling sometimes, hurrying on a bitter night past lighted windows full of manikins sporting Florida beach togs, but never before in her own home, where the Gauguin figures basked in the steamheated room.

Then she tried to concentrate on her inner

warmth. After all, she had a little furnace inside her. It could bring the temperature, all by itself, up to 98.6 degrees. No use, either. I can't keep warm by myself, she thought. She wanted coffee, but the electric stove was cold, too, no matter how many switches she turned.

We could break up the furniture and build a fire in the bathtub or some place, she thought in desperation, but realized that that wouldn't do, either, because the furniture was plastic and glass and chromium tubing.

She strained her ears for a sound in the pipes. Oh, that heavenly knocking that made so many apartment dwellers curse and turn over at six a.m., that wet-lipped whistle of escaping steam, that percolating sound that the radiator made when there was too much heat and it was turned off!

Her husband came in.

"Well?" she asked with stiff lips.

"No furnace in the building," he said. He also had difficulty in articulating. "Fellow from the tenth floor was down there, too. Couldn't find any superintendent or janitor. Lots of pipes, all cold."

"But where does the heat come from if there isn't any furnace?"

"Piped under the city streets. Comes for miles. Don't even know where the plant is."

"I never knew that." She looked at the radiator with increased foreboding. As long as she had thought that there was a furnace right downstairs – down twenty floors, to be sure, but still downstairs – she had felt that a fire could somehow certainly be started with something – telephone directories perhaps.

"Sure," said her husband. "You know, where you see the steam coming out of the manhole? I mean, where you used to see it."

"Then *nobody* has any heat?"

"Apparently not. I'm going out with this fellow from the tenth floor to see if we can locate the plant and find out what the chances are. How about some coffee first?"

She remembered then. "The electricity is off, too," she told him.

"Oh. That's why the elevator wasn't running when I came back up. It's the reason I was gone so long. I had to climb the stairs."

Mutely she thanked him. "I don't see why the

electricity has to go off just when there isn't any heat," she said peevishly.

"They make it out of coal."

She was dumbfounded. "Coal?" She had had an idea, she realized now, that wires ran from the switches directly to a lightning mine in a thundercloud over Bald Mountain. No, not quite that bad, but. . . . "If we only had a gas stove instead," she said.

"They make gas out of coal, too" said her husband. "I suppose that you never before thought back of a button on the wall or the knob on a radiator to the janitor, the scientist, the engineer, the trucks, the dynamos, the furnaces, the tugboats, the freighters, the railroads, the mines."

"Hush!" she cried, suddenly bursting into tears. "If it's that complicated, we'll never get warm." Her tears gushed hotly over her face for a moment, and then cold stung her wet skin. She dabbed at her cheeks with her mittens.

"You pushed a button, and said, let there be light, and there was light. I'll be back as soon as I find out anything," he added, and went out.

They were as helpless, she thought, as cave dwellers before fire was ever discovered. They were worse off, really, than the cave dwellers, who hadn't the memory of comfort to increase their misery. Before meat had ever been cooked, probably nobody minded eating it raw. As daylight faded, her mind spun fantasies in the gathering darkness. She thought back into that cold twilight of man's early history and tried to remember how fire had come. Rock striking against rock, was it? Tree branch rubbing against tree branch in the dry weather? No, it was believed now to have been lightning. Lightning from the lightning-mine in the cloud had come down and riven an oak and set the forest afire. Animals would have been trapped, roasted flesh tasted for the first time, live coals scooped like honey from the standing snags and carried home to the cave to be breathed upon and nourished with dry wood. So man had started his upward climb with the hearth and the forge.

Against her closed eyelids she imagined the green lizard look of the sky before the storm, the flare of white light over the landscape like the batting of an eyelid, the crack and rumble of thunder, and then in a spatter of rain the quick crackle of twigs curling in a fire, a hissing of steam from the green wood and of a flame against raindrops, and the advance – an unnoticed running in bleached grass and the bursting of a bush into red flower.

The picture took her back to a time when she had not turned a switch and set a thermostat and expected the dinner to cook at an even temperature. It is true, she had been hardly old enough to stem strawberries, but she could remember clearly the woodlot, the axes, the kitchen range with its box full of ashes, the chopping block and the box of kindling by the stove, the kerosene can and the lamps – though where the kerosene came from she had no idea even now. There were candles, too, but they were seldom used. She remembered a storeroom and candles in a box on the shelf. It was, actually, even less than a storeroom. It was simply an unused room in a big house inhabited by a small family. It was at the back of the house, on the second floor two doors beyond her own little room. She remembered now, too, how she had been awakened one night by voices in that room, hushed, taut voices. Her stomach had been knotted into a hard lump by fear. The voices could belong to no one except her parents, but what were they doing in that unused room in the middle of the night, talking so tensely? Up and out of bed she popped, in the cool summer night, in her sprigged cotton-crepe nightgown. Her feet remembered the feel of the matting in the hall to this moment, so vivid was the nightmare which turned out to be real, after all. Her parents turned from the window, and she saw the red glow behind the hill. Then her father went to dress, and rouse the men, and fight the fire with shovel and axe and fire itself – a fight that continued for days of ochre light and dropping ashes like grayed snow. But how was it that she had known, almost as soon as she had been put back to bed, that this was the work of wicked men? That was the nightmare, she remembered, that there were men evil enough to kindle wanton destruction. She saw them with scrubby beards and bloodshot eyes, slinking through blackberry brambles with their oily rags and tin boxes of matches. And that whole hill went up in resounding flame.

She dropped into a cold, confused sleep, in which the golden October roses and spiked red dahlias were made of fire, but sheathed in crystal so cold it burned the fingers.

She woke when her husband let himself into the

apartment sometime towards morning, but before the first glimmer of light appeared on the chromium. "The whole system has broken down," he said. "No coal coming out of the mines. Nobody knows just what's wrong." He lit a match and held it between his palms. It looked like a crown jewel, like all the wealth of the world.

"Let's go," she said. "Let's go where we chop our own wood and put it in the stove. There must be some place left like that."

AS THE YEARS PASSED, the memory of the fireless city had dwindled almost to the memory of a bad dream like the forest fire of her childhood. She lay on the ground, one morning, protected from the rough earth only by a tarpaulin and a spongy matting of grass, sheltered from the night air by several blankets. She woke and saw a filmy gray light, but no color. Could dawn be breaking already? At her right were the two little humps made by her children in their blankets; at her left lay the flat cocoon shed by her husband. A screen of bushes concealed the creek which murmured throatily over the boulders below them. She heard distinctly in the silence with its backdrop of water the clink of a pail on rock, the crumpling of paper, the breaking of twigs, then the sound of a match being struck and the burring sound of bees in the stove. Red light leapt on the tree trunks.

"This is the best moment of all my life," she whispered, and lay there watching the firelight. They had found the crude stove made of rocks and sheet iron in this prospector's camp yesterday afternoon. It had invited them to stay over night. The morning before had been joyful, the four of them setting out on a camping trip while the sun was still coming level across glittering pastures and smoky ponds, the two children singing, the mountains opening under their wheels. But this moment was better. She prolonged it until she could smell the coffee and bacon.

It was late afternoon when they rolled out of the foothills into a hot and dusty valley with fields of parched crops stretching dismally away from the road on either side. The wind had come up. They stopped at a general store with a red gasoline pump at one end of the porch. The man who filled their tank had a worried look on his face. Yes, it was bad weather. No rain for thirty days. All they needed was this wind and some damn fool with a cigarette. The ranger station on Green Mountain had just reported a smoke up Gold Creek Canyon. There was a pretty good chance of putting it out, but not if this wind took hold of it. Fire could jump fifty feet while you said *scat* on a wind like this.

She sat there, breathing painfully, waiting for the man to make change. Her husband got in and started the car. This was fear, again, but of a different sort. This time she felt her skin alternately flushed with blood and withered under cold sweat. This was fear of guilt.

"Are you sure you put the fire out?" she said to him finally, but in a low tone so that the children would not hear.

"Of course I am," he said irritably.

"They'll probably get it out all right," she said after a while. She knew he was as worried as she was. Still, they didn't know. It might not have been their fire. It might have been somebody who passed in a car and tossed a cigarette stub from the window. It might have been a happy-go-lucky pleasure seeker, or again a logging company working stealthily in hazardous weather, a log chain scraping on a log, or the men with oily rags. It couldn't, surely, have been the fire that cooked their coffee and bacon that morning? An unnoticed running through bleached grass, a snaking black line lying low until they were out of sight, and then darting up a tree trunk . . . to explode suddenly, the whole green top of the tree one giant torch burning out in the length of a gasp, and the embers on the wind sowing the mountains with flame.

The smoke hung in a yellow pall by day making the sun a sharp unnatural disc and blotting out the stars by night. The blaze provided its own illusion of bloody moonrise always behind the same hill. Then the wind rose, and it leapt, a dreaded crown fire, from tree top to tree top. Death followed under the red winds, and the prosperity of counties fell in a sifting of ashes. It swept into towns and out of them, leaving a black, corrugated rubble. It forced all before it down to the very beaches, where they lay, the four of them who had coffee and bacon in Gold Creek Canyon, and their neighbors, and a few Indians, and deer restlessly printing the sand with precise hooves, and cougars coughing and paying no attention to the deer, and wildcats, and one cow. Their tongues were thick with smoke and their eyes smarting. They all lay down on the strip of sand together between the ominous yellow gray surf at the edge of the world and the even more ominous yellow gray pall of smoke behind them. Everything burned.

HOW MUCH LATER was it that they came back? They had to start again right from the beginning. There was the land, to be sure, where their house had stood, and the already silvered snags which had once been a grove of firs, and the silver-purple lake of fireweed between them.

"This is it! Here's where the gate was. See?"

It was the daughter, almost grown up now. She had grown so much, nobody noticing, during the fire. The son was having an argument with his father over the possibility of catching a fish in the creek. The mother sat down on a stone that had been one of the gate-posts of that house they had built, which they had looked upon as a fortress in those days – after the Breakdown and before the Fire. She was too full of bitterness for tears. She sat scraping at the lumps of charcoal in the earth with the toe of one homemade deerskin moccasin. They had to start from scratch. It would be a cold night. She got up and walked toward where the house had stood. There it was – there was the only thing that remained, the chimney with a fireplace raised a little above the fireweed. Some of the hearthstones were still in place and projected in a shelf just below shoulder level. The thing looked like a pagan altar.

"Oh mother!" It was her daughter's voice. "We got a fish! and look! There's the fireplace all ready for us to use, and all we have to do is get a fire going and we can have dinner."

"Yes," said the mother."

COLOPHON

Three Fables was designed by the students enrolled in the winter and spring 1983 terms of Book Publishing: Fundamentals & Practice offered by Marylhurst College. The typography, by Irish Setter, is 12 point Bembo on 15 point leading with Albertus titling. All editions were printed on acid-free natural Accord paper by McNaughton & Gunn Lithographers of Ann Arbor, Michigan. The first printing consists of 1,300 copies of which 1,000 are sewn and wrapped with French cover jackets, 200 bound in linen over boards, and 100 handbound in linen over boards by Oregon Book Binding, numbered and signed by the author and publisher as a gift edition in celebration of the fifth anniversary of Breitenbush Publications.

The students and staff of *Book Publishing: Fundamentals & Practice* wish to express their gratitude to the following visiting lecturers:

David Godine, *Publisher*, David R. Godine Co., Boston, Massachusetts
Scott Walker, *Publisher,* Graywolf Press, Port Townsend, Washington
Martin White, *Typographer*, Irish Setter, Portland, Oregon
John Laursen, *Fine Printer/Designer*, Press-22, Portland, Oregon
Laurie Levich, *Cover Artist*, Portland, Oregon
August Frugé, *Director Emeritus*, U.C. Press, Berkeley, California
Gary Miranda, *Poet*, Portland, Oregon
Merritt Linn, *Novelist*, Portland, Oregon
Jean V. Naggar, *Literary Agent*, Manuscripts Unlimited, New York City
Daniel Kerr, *Commercial Printer*, Adprint Co., Portland, Oregon
Katherine McCanna, *Book Distributor*, Far West Book Service, Portland, Oregon
Richard Abel, *Publisher*, Timber Press, Portland, Oregon
Merl and Patti Miller, *Publishers*, Dilithium Press, Portland, Oregon
David Kherdian, *Novelist/Poet*, Aurora, Oregon
Nonny Hogrogian, *Book Illustrator*, Aurora, Oregon
Max Marbles, *Custom Book Binder*, Portland, Oregon
Jeanne Yeasting, *Editor*, U.W. Press, Seattle, Washington
Mary Ellen Rowe, *Representative*, St. Martins Press, New York City
Deborah Robboy, *Bookseller*, Catbird Seat Bookstore, Portland, Oregon

Our very special thanks to Miss Mary Barnard, Marylhurst Education Center, and the Metropolitan Arts Commission without whose assistance the publication of *Three Fables* would not have been possible.